First Publication, English

Maddison, London J. Mak the Kraken / London J. Maddison, Illustrated by Nick McCarthy.
Summary: An undiscovered species from the depths of the ocean, a Kraken named Mak,
ventures to the surface, overcoming the challenges of being different and following his dream
of interacting with people, finally achieving his goal with divers in a marine life refuge.

ISBN: 978-1-4834-6029-1 (sc)
ISBN:978-1-4834-6028-4 (e)

Lulu Publishing Services rev. date: 11/11/2016

Mak the Kraken

London J.
Maddison

Illustrated by
Nick McCarthy

Dedication:

To Chris, for his idea on a rainy El Nino morning in January and for introducing London J. Maddison to the most talented artist, Nick McCarthy. To Eric, Taylor and Mark who edit well and love the sea. To everyone who has been an inspiration to the author and illustrator. To children everywhere, whose imaginations spark new stories every day. . .and to our own Makai "Mak the Kraken".

Preface:

From the Author to Teachers, Conservation Instructors & Volunteers, Parents, and Children:

"We understand so much about the oceans through the brilliant study of marine biology and oceanography. Scientists discovered over 1,400 new species in the ocean in the year prior to the publishing of this book. The Smithsonian published an article and the California Academy of Sciences released a press release in June of 2015 stating that scientists celebrated World Ocean Day with more than 100 new species being discovered in a seven-week exploration of the Coral Triangle off the Philippines. Though there are many new and amazing discoveries in the depths of the seas every year, there are creatures in the oceans that we have never seen. It is the curiosity and intrigue about those mysteries of the vast waters of the earth that have prompted us to explore, but according to NOAA, less than 5% of our oceans have been discovered, with as much as 95% still remaining undiscovered. There are thought to be thousands of creatures we have never encountered abiding in the depths of our waters. These are creatures that are different from

anything we have seen….and that is where we find the inspiration for the story of Makai "Mak" the Kraken.

In the interest of conservation, 5% of the profits of this book will be donated to ocean education organizations including, but not limited to, the Monterey Bay Aquarium, the Long Beach Aquarium, the Birch Aquarium at Scripps Institution of Oceanography, UC San Diego; and the Ocean Institute in Dana Point, California for the furthering of ocean education for children and adults of all ages.

The Kraken were once the most secret and misunderstood creatures in all of the Seven Seas. Fishermen, pirates, sailors and even marine scientists didn't really believe in them. Most landlubbers thought of them as frightening myths. They were named Kraken to mean a giant sea monster, shown mainly in drawings to appear like a twisted octopus or giant squid attacking ships and sailors. There were legends of people seeing them off the coasts of Norway and Greenland, destroying pirate ships and fishing boats.

No one knew the Kraken were shy, kind creatures, living deep in the undiscovered parts of the ocean, along with hundreds of other living things we've never seen. The older Kraken told legends and stories in the hidden caves of the ocean to help the young Kraken learn. They had to tell many stories about ships and humans, because the young Kraken had dreams of becoming friends with people and needed to know the danger. These Kraken tales were enough to frighten most shy, young Kraken and stop them from going to the surface, but they didn't scare Makai. . . a brave Kraken known as "Mak" the Kraken.

Until Mak began to venture to the surface of the ocean, humans hadn't seen many of his kind. It might have been Mak's octopus-like head, bright orange and yellow speckled skin, gigantic size and long tentacles that seemed fearsome. It could have been his hypnotizing song that was mysteriously familiar. Maybe it was because the other Kraken rarely went to the surface that people would find Mak so terrifying.

Mak was different than the other Kraken. He dreamed of meeting people just as the other young Kraken did, but he was brave enough to follow his dream when he was very young. Because of his curiosity and determination to make friends with humans, Mak tried, almost daily, to venture to the water's surface to find people. Mak would wake up every morning, swim out of his sea cave in the depths of the sea and glide up, up, up until he was just under the water's surface, to look for the hull of a ship. Most days he was patient in his search, and found at least one ship to visit. As he approached a ship, he would carefully lift one eye out of the water, just above the surface, to peek at the ship and see if it were filled with fishermen, sailors, pirates or scientists. He had to be careful because each group of people treated him in a different way if they caught a glimpse of him.

Mak had seen the legends come to life in his trips to the surface of the water, just as his parents and grandparents had told. If it was a pirate ship, he could expect them to shoot their cannons at him in case he was trying to steal their treasure.

If it was a fishing boat, he could expect harpoons to be launched at him in hopes that they could bring him back for dinner (and not as a guest). If it was a sailing vessel he would expect them to call in the Coast Guard to figure out what to do with him. But if it was a science exploration, he thought they would want to capture the Kraken to study him. Mak knew the scientists helped marine life. He had heard stories about them taking injured seals to places on land to get well. There were legends of people tagging and releasing sea lions back into the water and Mak wondered if they would tag and release him.

No Kraken had ever been caught and he did not want to be the first, but young Mak, like his young Kraken friends, dreamed of the company of humans. They longed to be a part of communities of people and hoped to become friends with a human child. But the Kraken are peaceful and shy, and most are not brave enough to follow that dream as a young Kraken. Sadly, at the age of twelve, the Kraken all change their dreams and lose the hope of being friends with people. . . **FOREVER**. At age twelve even the braver Kraken will return to the depths of the ocean, giving up the idea of this oddly matched friendship. If they do go to the surface after the age of twelve, just for a glimpse of the sunshine, sea birds and waves above the ocean's surface, they do so with the whales and dolphins, but away from the hulls of ships for fear of cannons, harpoons and nets.

On his fourth birthday, Mak went to the surface and secretly ventured all the way to land, to the end of a pier where he saw a flock of seagulls and a child fishing with her father. He ever so carefully put one eye out of the water and then the other. He tried to hide his huge body with just his eyes and large forehead showing above the surface, and slowly glided over to the fishing line and into the sight of the happy little girl.

"I'm catching something Papa, but what is it?" asked the little girl pointing at Mak in total excitement. She had a big smile on her face, but her unsuspecting father was turned toward shore with his back to the ocean, baiting his hook. As the father turned around he gasped in fear, seeing Mak's outline through the crystal clear water. He grabbed the girl, dropping the fishing pole into the ocean right on Mak's forehead, and ran down the pier to the shore. In the distance Mak could hear the father's voice.

"That's a terrible, ugly sea monster, honey" he said, "We need to get away"... And that was all the Kraken could hear except the little girl saying… "I think it was nice".

Sad and lonely, hurt and disappointed, Mak dove back underwater into the deep sea. He had never seen his reflection, but knew what ugly meant. He had seen other Kraken, who he thought were beautiful creatures. He knew the man had told that sweet little girl that Mak was ugly and different, but didn't understand how that could be. He knew that he was not ugly inside—he was filled with love for people no matter how they treated him and found joy in every adventure. Mak thought about the little girl and her father, and decided that maybe humans were like Kraken and wanted to be friends only before the age of twelve as well. Mak curled up in his cave amidst the seagrass, hugging the anchor he had been given as a baby from his mother and the lobster pot he had found in the winter, and he almost cried.

For the next seven years, Mak faithfully followed his dream and continued to try to befriend a human. Adventure after adventure he failed. His skin was scarred from the harpoons of fishermen, one of his tentacles was broken at the tip from a cannonball fired from a pirate ship and his heart was heavy. He knew his twelfth birthday was only a few weeks away and that he would dive to the depths of the ocean forever, giving up hope of befriending a human, as all Kraken did at age twelve. Nearly eight years of trying to fulfill his dream had passed since he saw the little girl at the pier. As he began to lose hope, he curled up in his cave amidst the seagrass, hugging the anchor and the lobster pot, and this time he did cry, but only for a little while.

Mak just couldn't give up on his dream. On the eve of his twelfth birthday, Mak was determined to make a human friend. Mak wanted to change the myth that Kraken were sea monsters. . . *FOREVER*. In a moment of brilliance, Mak had an idea about how to make his dream come true.

This was an idea that he could never tell any other Kraken…not his mother, his father, his grandmother, his sister or his friends, because they would all stop him. So on that very eve of his twelfth birthday, after years of being treated terribly by people, his nature of patience and tolerance drove Mak to make a big decision.

He knew where the marine biology and science boats gathered this time of year near the shore, and decided to find them and to do what no Kraken had ever done before. His idea was to get caught and be taken back to be studied and tagged. That way he could show them his gentle friendship and meet the people. He could get that chance he wanted to befriend a human, even if it was in a science laboratory. But because of conservation, and the bravery of Mak the Kraken, that's not at all what happened.

Mak boldly swam into the waves, under the surfers and paddlers to the shallows where the small marine biology boats were sampling the water quality of the ocean. He went daringly close to shore…closer than ever before. The end of a pier had been his closest encounter to land at age four, but now he was so close he could see the shells on the sandy bottom. As he looked toward shore, Mak was distracted from his mission of trying to get caught when he saw something he had never seen before. Something wonderful. It was a group of humans, but they were under the water. The humans were both small and large, covered in an underwater suit and helmet, with tanks on their backs. The tanks let them breathe under the water, causing bubbles to float up all around them, and they were holding a ray of light. It seemed that the larger people were showing the smaller ones the fish in the sea.

Mak was very happy to see humans under the water. Maybe they could be friends underwater rather than out of the water, where it would be easier for him to move and breath in his natural habitat. He slowly approached the divers, who were unarmed—no guns, no harpoons and no nets, just a flashlight and small fish swimming around them.

As the humans saw him, the larger ones drew back in fear, turned and swam for the shore, leaving the small two staring at him. "Kraken parents would never leave their young in danger like that" Mak thought, but he was glad they did.

The two young humans had masks over their faces, but their eyes were fixed upon Mak. He gently reached out a tentacle toward one of the small divers and touched him on the gloved hand. Then he slowly recoiled his tentacle and made the only sound a Kraken can make, which sounds exactly like a song of the sea. He sang his humming tune with a soothing, delightful melody that is very close to the tune 'New Britain" know best as the song "Amazing Grace". The young divers stared, smiling eagerly, unafraid of Mak, but still motionless except for the slow rising and falling of the waves and the ocean's current. Mak again reached out a tentacle and touched the boy as the girl watched. The boy touched Mak's tentacle with his other hand and a gave a muffled "He's nice" which gurgled underwater through his air tube.

Mak was overjoyed. He had finally made contact with humans who did not fear him.

In a moment, Mak's happiness and sense of accomplishment vanished as he looked up in horror. The adult divers had come back to save the children, and now carried spear guns. Seeing that the Kraken was touching both children under the sea, they thought that Mak was planning to coil around them to eat them, ugly sea monster that they assumed he was. They aimed their spear guns at him, but the boy and girl were too close to Mak for them to shoot. When Mak started to slowly back away from the young divers, the boy and the girl moved in front of him, between the adults with the spear guns and the Kraken. As they couldn't really talk under the water, they motioned to the adults waving their hands and shaking their heads "no" so that they would not hurt the Kraken. In Mak's mind, the boy and girl risked their lives to protect him, saving him with their own lives, which was a very noble thing for them to do.

As the adult divers began to see that the children weren't in danger, Mak ventured a little closer. One of the adults had a large belt with a metal panel on it. Mak saw a Kraken on the reflective panel and wondered why the belt had a Kraken emblem on it. In a few minutes, Mak realized, after some movement, that he was looking at a reflection of himself. He looked like all the other Kraken, but his colors were much different. He was vivid orange and yellow. His orange was like a reef of bright coral or a Garibaldi, the yellows were like a Moorish Idol instead of dark blue tones of the other Kraken.

The adult divers were defensive and careful, but when Mak reached his tentacle out as a gesture of friendship, the diver put out her hand and touched it. Mak, once again, began his humming tune and the diver smiled, as the children had. After quite a long time and many moments of reaching out, the divers had to return to the shore. They didn't try to hurt him or catch him, they just waved their hands and swam away. Mak waved his tentacles, mimicking their waves as a gesture of friendship.

What Mak didn't know as he headed back to his underwater cave that night, was that the bay and shoreline where he had discovered the divers was a marine life sanctuary. It was a place where no ocean creature, shell or even piece of kelp or coral could be harmed or taken. He didn't know that the spear guns that the adult divers brought to try to protect their children were just tranquilizers that were only allowed to be used in self-defense in the sanctuary against sharks, or to carefully save a hurt or injured sea creature.

After meeting the people, Mak told his story to the other Kraken. After meeting Mak, the divers told the story of the Kraken, to teach people about Mak the Kraken and the importance of the marine life sanctuary. Mak soon learned that it was a place of refuge for all the living creatures of the ocean and provided them with a haven where people and sea life could swim together and learn about each other. This sanctuary was a place of conservation, set aside to preserve the coast and marine life which allowed the Kraken safety.

Almost every day, Mak would wake up, leave his sea cave in the deepest part of the ocean and rise to the surface, gliding into the marine life sanctuary to search for his friends, the divers. He would usually find them on Saturdays, but every other day of the week he would find other divers who had heard about the Kraken, all seeking to meet Mak and hear his beautiful song. Sometimes Mak would bring other Kraken to get to know the people, like his grandfather who loved adventure or his little sister, who was very brave for her age.

Mak the Kraken had done what no Kraken had done before. He went back to the depths of the ocean and shared stories with all of the Kraken about his adventures with people every day. The Kraken were proud of Mak, having followed the childhood dream of every Kraken. Mak had shown the Kraken that if you keep trying, and don't give up, you can fulfill your dreams.

Although Mak did an amazing thing for the Kraken and people, the humans also did something just as wonderful for the Kraken. They went back and wrote the story of Mak the Kraken so that all of mankind could know that these were not sea monsters, but kind and good sea creatures that were just unfamiliar and different. The two adult divers that had first met Mak with the children shared the story with world. They educated people that the Kraken were friendly creatures and should be biologically protected from any kind of harm, like whales and dolphins. They made sure to share that the Kraken were definitely not edible like squid and octopus. More people began to teach more people about the oceans and the many creatures within them, which encouraged scientists to explore further into the ocean's depths for creatures we have not seen.

From the eve of Mak's twelfth birthday, the Kraken and humans were friends, helping each other in the storms of the sea and communicating by song. The Kraken warned surfers when sharks were in the water, warned ships of icebergs, swam in the way of pirate ships to stop their plunder and pillaging and helped sailors and the Coast Guard.

Once a feared sea monster, the Kraken had turned into man's greatest living ocean resource and friend. The Kraken had taught humans not to judge or fear something just because it is different. They had taught mankind that what might be most feared for its size or appearance, may actually be a friend and a great hero who saves the lives of thousands.

For Mak's bravery and persistence, he was honored by humans and the Kraken forever. At the site on the shore of Mak's first meeting with the divers, at the edge of the marine life sanctuary, a statue of his exact size and color stands in his honor. Unlike the statues of mermaids, dolphins and starfish that stand on the shores of our Seven Seas, Mak the Kraken's statue has a plaque below it with these words:

In Honor of Mak the Kraken, who visits often and
will live forever on the shore of this refuge and
in the hearts of all who know his story.

Follow your dreams…
Accept those who are different…
Conserve the resources of the earth and oceans…

Look out to the marine life sanctuary, and into your heart.
Here and there you will find Mak the Kraken.

Glossary:

Conservation: The action of preservation, protection or restoration of the natural environment, natural ecosystems, vegetation and wildlife.

Deep Sea: The lowest layer in the ocean at a depth of 1800 meters or more where little or no light penetrates. Initially, scientists assumed that life would be sparse, but we have now discovered that life is abundant in the deep ocean.

Garibaldi: A species of bright orange fish in the damselfish family in the subtropical northeastern part of the Pacific Ocean. The official marine state fish of the state of California.

Habitat (or natural habitat): An area inhabited by a particular species of plant, animal or other organism that provides it food and shelter as well as a community of like species. Habitat refers to the environmental area surrounding the species. Ocean fish, such as tuna, need salt water habitats whereas freshwater fish, such as trout, need fresh water and neither could live in the other's habitat. For example, humans cannot live underwater because they need air, but they can dive with a tank under water for short periods of time to explore the ocean habitat.

Kraken: A legendary sea monster that is not a sea monster at all, but a kind friendly ocean creature. Historically pirates blamed Kraken for mishaps at sea when they had no other way of explaining losing/sinking a ship or misplacing their stolen cargo (because they couldn't always remember what happened).

Landlubber: A person unfamiliar with the sea or sailing.

Laboratory: (Lab) A laboratory is a facility that provides equipment and the needed for scientific and technological research, experiments and measurement.

New Britain/Amazing Grace: The tune of a 1779 Christian hymn which was joined to the words in 1835 by William Walker in the U.S., which is the tune it is sung to today. It is one of the most recognizable songs in the English-speaking world, often a song of the sea heard on ships.

Marine Life Sanctuary: A place along the ocean and beach where all sea life and beach life, including birds as well as shells, rocks and all natural plants and sea life are protected. People can't take or catch anything, but are usually allowed to visit, look at the marine life and dive in the water to see the marine life. These sanctuaries are places of refuge for all the ocean's resources and living creatures. There are many different designations depending on the country or state you are in.

Norway and Greenland: Norway is a country bordering Sweden, Finland, Russia, the Skagerrak Strait and with territory including the western portion of the Scandinavian Peninsula and the island Jan Mayen as well as the archipelago of Svalbard. Norway has an extensive coastline along the North Atlantic Ocean and the Barents Sea. Until 1814 the territory included the Faroe Islands, Greenland and Iceland. **Greenland** is a country, considered the world's largest island, located between the Arctic and Atlantic Oceans. The nearest countries to Greenland are Canada and Iceland. The Capitol is Nuuk. Greenland contains the world's largest national park, Northeast Greenland National Park and 75% of the country is covered by ice.

The Seven Seas: The term "the Seven Seas" is defined differently across history and across the world. It is an ancient term that means all of the world's oceans, which make up 71% of the earth's surface. Saline water covers 72% of the earth's surface due to other water bodies filled with salt water and called "seas". Since the 19th century, the term "the Seven Seas" has meant the Arctic, North Atlantic, South Atlantic, Indian, North Pacific, South Pacific and Southern (or Antarctic) Ocean. Many references do not split the north and south Atlantic and north and south Pacific, so this equals five seas when combined. These are the largest seas, making up more than 135 million square miles of surface water, reaching to depths of over 30,000 feet. The International Hydrographic Association, based in Monaco, indicates additional bodies of salt water (saying there are 70 worldwide). These include the Mediterranean Sea, Caribbean Sea, South China Sea, Gulf of Mexico, Okhotsk Sea, East

China Sea, Hudson Bay, Japan Sea, Andaman Sea, North Sea, Red Sea and Baltic Sea, among others.

According to NOAA, (the National Oceanic and Atmospheric Administration in the USA), only 5% of the oceans worldwide have been explored. This leaves 95% unexplored.

Tranquilizer: A drug that causes tranquility and sedates an animal to make them calm and sleepy. Tranquilizer guns are used to temporarily calm animals in both captive and wild settings if they are in harm's way or if they are putting a person in danger, such as a lion at the zoo, and in the wild, so that the animal can be handled safely without being harmed.

About the Author:

As a certified planner by the American Institute of Certified Planners (AICP) and a LEED Accredited Professional, the author has written about sustainability and the environment for over 30 years with over 300 published articles, documents and stories. London J. Maddison is a pseudonym used to separate professional and fiction writing careers. The author, a first generation American of British heritage, works and resides in California and Hawaii.

Additional publications by London J. Maddison are in various stages of the publishing process. To connect on social media please visit:

London J. Maddison on Facebook: https://www.facebook.com/profile.php?id=100011412121704

Linked In: https://www.linkedin.com/in/london-j-maddison-5616a0114

Twitter: @LondonJMaddison
Twitter: @MaktheKraken

Artist Biography:

Nicholas (Nick) McCarthy is a San Francisco, California Bay Area local, living in Concord, CA. Nick attended California State University, Monterey Bay where he received a Bachelor of Arts Degree in Mixed Media Design. Nick specializes in illustration, focusing on pointillism and realism. He is involved in exhibitions all around Northern California and across the country, having illustrations at the National Steinbeck Center in Salinas and the Bedford Gallery in Walnut Creek, CA. Some of these book illustrations have been featured in past and will be featured in future exhibitions. Nick can be contacted at nick5036@gmail.com or through his website: https://nicholasmccarthy@allyounet/4975584